You Have Ghost Mail

Terence Blacker is a successful writer of fiction for children and adults. His *Ms Wiz* series of books has been widely translated and his children's novel *The Transfer* is being developed for TV. He lives in a farmhouse on the Suffolk–Norfolk border and when he's not writing he plays the guitar, writes songs and scores goals for his local football team.

"Macmillan's Shock Shop range is a bit of a find – a series of really thrilling stories, spookily presented and written by top-class authors. Here, Terence Blacker . . . has come up with a cunning and creepy story . . . gripping stuff" *Guardian*

"Scary and dramatic" *TES*

D1392026

Shock Shop is a superb collection of short, illustrated, scary books for younger readers by some of today's most acclaimed writers for children.

Other titles in Shock Shop:

The Bodigulpa Jenny Nimmo
Stealaway K. M. Peyton
Hairy Bill Susan Price
Long Lost Jan Mark
Goodbye, Tommy Blue Adèle Geras
The Beast of Crowsfoot Cottage Jeanne Willis
Wicked Chickens Vivian French

SHOCK SHOP

You Have Ghost Mail

Terence Blacker

Illustrated by Adam Stower

MACMILLAN CHILDREN'S BOOKS

First published 2002 by Macmillan Children's Books

This edition published 2003 by Macmillan Children's Books
a division of Macmillan Publishers Limited
20 New Wharf Road, London N1 9RR
Basingstoke and Oxford
www.panmacmillan.com

Associated companies throughout the world

ISBN 0 330 39699 4

Text copyright © Terence Blacker 2002
Illustrations copyright © Adam Stower 2002

The right of Terence Blacker and Adam Stower to be identified as
the author and illustrator of this work has been asserted by them
in accordance with the Copyright, Designs and Patents Act 1988.

3 5 7 9 8 6 4 2

A CIP catalogue record for this book is available from
the British Library.

Typeset by Intype London Ltd
Printed and bound in Great Britain by Mackays of Chatham plc, Kent

Contents

Chapter 1
The Message

It was dark outside, and very still.

In the walnut tree near the house of Matthew Bourne, a tawny owl shrieked, its harsh hunting cry cutting the night air before silence descended once more.

The house itself slumbered, making only the sounds that a s l u m b e r i n g house will make. A fridge shuddered into life. A grandfather clock ticked. The sudden urgent scrabbling behind a skirting board betrayed the presence of a mouse.

Upstairs, in the bedroom of Matthew Bourne, son of Stephen Bourne, brother of Catherine Bourne, something stirred.

Matthew had always been a good sleeper. He had learned to trust the peace of the countryside around Walnut Tree Farm to ease him into slumber at even the most difficult, the saddest of times. When his mother was taken from them four years ago, Matthew would often escape from the pain and loneliness by closing his eyes and sleeping.

So tonight Matthew had no idea that, within his room, not far from where he slept, other less familiar night noises could be heard. A click. An uncertain crackle. The sounds of electricity coming to life.

Across the room, the screen of Matthew's new computer began to glow in the darkness. The light it shed was unlike that of normal computers. It was blood-red.

After a few seconds, a small dark smudge appeared at the bottom of the screen. It rose, slowly and silently, like a bubble. When it reached the centre of the screen it stayed uncertainly, swaying slightly. Seconds later, another dark mark appeared. It also moved slowly upwards and settled at the centre of the screen. Then another, and another.

The four shapes hung there for several seconds. Then, like a memory slowly returning to the mind, they began to become sharper and more focused until, unmistakably, they spelled out a single word.

help

After an hour, the image began to fade – first the letters, then the background, until only a small stain of red remained at the centre of the screen. Then that too disappeared and the computer was once more dark, silent and untroubled.

Outside, a rabbit screamed as a fox pounced, its sharp and deadly teeth closing on its victim's neck.

And Matthew Bourne slept on.

Chapter 2
A Bad Feeling

Matthew knew a bit about computers.

He had surfed the Net at school. He had sent emails to his best friend Angie Wright from his sister Catherine's computer at home. Now and then he could help his father when he was having a problem on the ancient machine used for the farm accounts.

So, when he was given an Epsilon 460 one Saturday late in October on his tenth birthday, he was able to set it up and get it going that evening without any problems.

It was on Sunday morning that things started going wrong.

Matthew had gulped down his breakfast and hurried back to his bedroom. His father

was already out on the farm somewhere and Catherine was still asleep when he logged on to the new computer and prepared to make e-contact with Angie.

The computer had seemed to be working more slowly than yesterday, as if it were having difficulty waking up. Then, just after he had started his email, something strange happened.

Hi. Angie

Matthew had written.

This is me, Matto123. What d'you think of that for a screen name? I got the idea

At that point, the screen froze. Matthew tapped several times on the keyboard. At first nothing happened. Then the letters of his email seemed to tremble and vibrate, almost as if there were something behind them, within the computer, that was pushing to get through. As Matthew stared at the screen, a tiny dot became visible, pulsing slowly, growing larger, slowly and almost imperceptibly.

It was a single word.

help

Matthew tapped once more. Nothing. He attempted to delete the email. But it was as if the computer had taken on a life of its own.

Matthew stood up. He backed away from
the computer, out of the room and down
the corridor. Knocking once, he entered
Catherine's room. All that could be seen of his
sister was a mop of dark hair poking out of
the top of the duvet.

"Cath." Matthew spoke uncertainly, knowing that Catherine was never at her best in the
morning.

A low rumble, acknowledging him but not

entirely friendly, came from within the folds of the bed.

"When you're on your computer, right, have you ever been writing something when something strange appears on the screen?"

"Go away, you brat."

"Like, a word you haven't typed?"

"What?" A hand emerged and slowly lowered the duvet. Catherine opened her eyes and looked up at her brother. "What kind of word?"

"It looks a bit like . . . 'help'. It's weird. You should see it."

Catherine sat up, swung her legs out of bed and began walking towards the door. "This had better not be one of your jokes," she muttered.

Moments later she was standing in front of the computer. The screen showed an email, half written, and nothing else.

"I don't understand," said Matthew. "It was there a moment ago."

"You are dead." Catherine turned and

stumbled back to the door. "When I wake up, you are officially going to be well and truly dead." From the corridor, she called back, "Don't bother Dad with this either."

Alone, Matthew sat on the side of his bed. He looked warily at the present for which he had waited so long but which now seemed oddly threatening. Catherine had been right about one thing. Normally when he had a problem, Matthew would turn to his father, but the last thing Mr Bourne needed was the news that Matthew's birthday present was sending him weird messages of its own accord. He had enough on his mind already. The farm was in difficulty and money was tight.

Angie, on the other hand, might be able to help. She may have been only ten years old, but there were few adults who knew more about the tricks that computers played than Angie Wright. In class, she was a bit of a joke – "Mouse", they called her, not only because she was small and nervous-looking but also because, whenever she had a spare moment, she seemed to be in front of a screen, her hand on the mouse of a computer. In a sense, that was why she and Matthew had become friends. They were both, in their own ways, outsiders.

Matthew sat down once more. He deleted his last email and started again.

Hi. Angie
What d'you think of my screen-name. Matto123? Cool or what? I think I might have a bit of a weird machine here. I was just writing you an email whe

The screen froze. The letters began to tremble. "Not again." Matthew spoke out loud and, as his words hung in the air, he was aware of the faint prickle of alarm at the back of his neck.

11

He sat back as the image grew on the screen. It was two words this time, and they seemed larger than before:

help me

Nervously, his hands clammy with sweat, Matthew reached for the "Off" button. He pressed it once and the screen went dark.

"Help? Help me?" Angie laughed, a weird, slightly mad giggle, when, moments later, Matthew reached her on the telephone.

"It's not a joke, Angie," said Matthew. "Then when I got my sister to have a look, there was nothing there. She thinks I'm losing it."

"Maybe it's some kind of screen-saver thing. Or a pop-up ad. I bet it's nothing to worry about."

Matthew sighed. "It's kind of scary," he said. "Come and see for yourself if you don't believe me . . ."

"Hang on."

Matthew heard a brief conversation between Angie and her mother. Their house was some ten kilometres away from Walnut Tree Farm and Mrs Wright seemed none too anxious to be a taxi-driver that day. But when Angie wanted something badly enough, she tended to get her own way.

Soon she was back on the line. "I'll see you later." She sighed dramatically, almost like a parent. "I've got a really bad feeling about you and computers."

Chapter 3
wearenotalone.com

The Bourne family did not receive many visitors. Walnut Tree Farm was situated some way from the village but that was not the main reason for the lack of callers. Since the tragedy, the Bournes had seemed to have fewer friends. "That poor family," people in the village would say, shaking their heads and keeping their distance, as if misfortune were a disease, something you could catch.

The tragedy? If you came from those parts, no explanation was necessary. Just under four years ago, ten days before Christmas, Gemma Bourne, the young wife of Stephen and mother of Catherine and Matthew, had been driving home from work one wet and blustery

14

evening when her car was hit by a lorry on the main road. It was not the crash that killed her, police reported later, but the fact that the car had rolled from the road, ending upside-down in a flooded ditch. Gemma Bourne, unable to escape, had drowned.

For a while after the funeral, local people had decided that the best and kindest way to support the three remaining members of the Bourne family was to let them grieve in peace. But gradually, leaving them in peace somehow became a habit. When Stephen sold off a couple of fields to allow him more time with his children, the village agreed that it was a sensible idea but, secretly, there were murmurings that the farmer was becoming rather odd.

It seemed a bit unnatural, some of the villagers said – the way Mr Bourne collected Matthew at the end of the day, hugging him at the school gate, but saying little to the other waiting parents. Catherine, who took the bus to a secondary school further away, was said to be causing problems in class. People began to remember Gemma Bourne as a sunnier, more normal person than she had ever been. They saw the family left behind as slightly strange, aloof – embarrassing in a way that was difficult to explain.

All this meant that when, later that afternoon, the bell at the farm's front door rang and Sandra Wright and her daughter stood on the doorstep, it was something of a surprise.

Mr Bourne had cooked a fry-up for the children's Sunday lunch and the kitchen was more of a mess than usual, with muddy gumboots near the door, unwashed dishes piled high in the sink, a smell of bacon in the air.

"Oh hi, Angie." Stephen Bourne stood back and opened the door. "Hello, Mrs Wright. Come in."

Angie's mother smiled. "Sandy, please."

"Come to admire Matthew's computer?" Stephen asked Angie.

"Admire. Er, yes, that's right," said Angie rather too quickly to be convincing.

"He's upstairs."

As Angie made her way towards the stairs, she heard her mother say, "When should I collect her?"

"Any time," Mr Bourne said. "Unless . . . you fancied staying for a coffee?"

Upstairs, Angie pushed at Matthew's door. He had drawn the curtains and sat motionless, shoulders slumped, in front of the screen.

"How's the freaky 'puter?" Angie asked.

Matthew nodded at the screen in front of him. "I'm online," he said. "But every time I try to email anyone, I get the old 'help me' message."

"Weird." Angie pulled up a stool, then took a pillow from Matthew's bed so that, when she sat down, she was on the same level as he was. "Let me have a go."

As Matthew moved aside, she took over the controls, her eyes locking on to the screen, her

hand closing on the computer mouse, so that she seemed a small, human part of the machine.

"Reboot and log on again," Angie murmured to herself, tapping the keyboard and clicking the mouse. She sat back for a moment. "This machine seems very slow," she said.

"It was quicker yesterday," said Matthew.

"Maybe something zapped you – some kind of computer virus. That's why the system's so slow and why you're getting your strange messages." She moved the mouse and double-clicked. "I'm running a virus check."

Matthew looked confused. Sometimes when Angie was in front of a computer, she seemed to be speaking a whole new language.

"It's like a little medical check-up but for computers," she said, her eyes fixed on the screen.

After a few moments, a sign appeared. It read: NO VIRUS DETECTED.

"Nothing wrong there." Angie sighed and sat back, folding her arms. "Maybe these messages are some kind of pop-up ad."

From downstairs in the kitchen came the sound of adult laughter. Matthew glanced at Angie and they both seemed about to say something but then thought better of it.

"What kind of ad asks me to help it all the time?" Matthew stood up to switch on the light. "Maybe I should call the shop and ask them about it."

"And it's not just when you send emails," said Angie quietly.

Matthew turned to look at the screen. There, at its centre, obscuring the sign which read NO VIRUS DETECTED, was a small cloud of red, its edges fuzzy and undefined. As it grew in size, two words began to form within it.

"Here we go," murmured Matthew.

But this time the message was different.

For a moment, Matthew and Angie stared at the screen in silence. Then, as if the computer had somehow taken on a life of its own and could overhear them, Angie whispered, "All right, I'll admit it. That is a bit spooky."

"Who's Jenny and why's she creeping?" said Matthew, fear in his voice.

"It's no computer malfunction, that's for sure," said Angie. She took off her glasses and wiped the lenses with a tissue, blinking as she did so.

Angie with her face undressed always startled Matthew. She looked oddly helpless, like a lost mole. "You could call the computer shop and tell them your new Epsilon's sending you weird messages," she said, then frowned. "On the other hand, maybe not. They'll think you're a nutter."

Matthew sighed. "Trust me to have a haunted computer."

21

Angie returned her glasses to their rightful place. "Help. Help me. Creeping Jenny. It's almost as if we're being given clues."

"Maybe it's some kind of game that's part of the computer. We've activated it by mistake."

Angie shook her head. "I checked that," she said.

"Dad's going to be so annoyed," Matthew muttered. "He saved up for ages."

Angie looked up suddenly. "What did you say a moment ago?"

"It's my dad. We've been talking about this—"

"No, before that. About the computer being haunted."

"It was a joke, Angie."

But Angie had stood up and was gouging in the back pocket of her jeans. She took out a handful of frayed, dirty-looking paper which she laid carefully on the desk beside the computer. It was cuttings from newspapers – stories that had caught the attention of her strange, jackdaw mind. "I collect stuff," she explained as she looked through them. When she reached the fifth, scuffed bit of paper, she held it up triumphantly and passed it to Matthew.

"*Are Mobile Phones Calling Up Ghosts?*" Matthew read the headline and laughed. "You're not telling me you believe this stuff, are you?"

"Just read it," said Angie.

Matthew shrugged and read the cutting out loud. "*Britain's ghosts are being disturbed by the explosion in mobile phone and computer use, experts in the paranormal believe. Incidents of ghost sightings, poltergeists, even of haunted electronic equipment, have increased dramatically over the past three years. The reason for this phenomenon, it is* *claimed, is intense electromagnetic and microwave radiation caused by 39 million-plus cellphones and computers. 'We believe that frequencies used by modern technology have disturbed the spirit world,' says Brian Wainwright of the Psychic Society, reporting on research with SpIDER, or the Spontaneous Incident Data Electronic Recorder. 'We're not saying that people should be alarmed, but the spirit world has definitely been disturbed by the new technology. Anyone who has experienced an encounter of the paranormal kind is asked to contact the Psychic Society on their website <u>wearenotalone.com</u>'."*

Matthew gave the cutting back to Angie. "You don't think . . ." he said, glancing nervously at the screen where the red cloud still shimmered with its message.

"I don't know," said Angie. "It—"

There was a light knock at the door and Angie's mother walked in.

"Time to go, love," she said. "You can come

over and see Matthew's computer some other time."

"Good," said Angie, moving to stand beside Matthew in front of the computer, trying to look natural.

Her mother frowned. "What's been going on?" she asked.

"Nothing, Mum."

Mrs Wright stepped forward and parted Matthew and Angie as if she were looking through curtains. "Hm, nothing much there."

"Eh?" Matthew turned. The screen innocently showed its sign, NO VIRUS DETECTED – and nothing else.

"You two have been up to something," said Angie's mother.

Angie was folding her newspaper cuttings. "You're so suspicious, Mum," she said, putting them back in her pocket. "See you, Matto." She smiled at Matthew and winked briefly from behind her glasses. "Don't forget to check out that website I told you about."

Matthew heard the front door close downstairs. He sat down in front of his computer, clicked on to the Internet and tapped out http://www.wearenotalone.com

After a few seconds, letters appeared on the screen in bright and jaunty colours. They read,

THIS IS wearenotalone.com THE PSYCHIC SOCIETY'S OWN WEB PAGE WHERE THE MOST EXCITING NEWS IN PARANORMAL RESEARCH BREAKS FIRST. WELCOME TO ALL VISITORS FROM THE HUMAN AND THE SPIRIT WORLD.

"Oh, please," Matthew murmured.

He looked down the list of contents: *Psychic Investigators Meet at Copenhagen Conference*; *Poltergeist Activity Reported in Maine, USA*; *New SpIDER Model to be Available Next Year*; *Paranormal Reports from PS Members Around the World*; *New Research Links Ghost Boom to New Technology*. He was about to move the cursor when he noticed something odd.

The letters of the wearenotalone.com website were becoming indistinct – or, rather, they were swaying backwards and forwards, almost as if Matthew were looking at them through a film of water. As he watched, the letters became more difficult to read until the whole screen appeared flooded, as if it were awash with water. It was so convincing that Matthew found himself reaching out to check that his computer had not been flooded somehow. Its surface was dry and warm.

He moved his hand towards the power switch but then hesitated. At that moment, for some reason, it felt wrong to close down the computer. For a minute or so he gazed, as if hypnotized.

Then he seemed to come to his senses. Shaking his head at the never-ending strangeness of his new computer, he pressed the switch, stood up and went downstairs.

Chapter 4
An Eye in the Night

Maybe it was because he had been unable to eat much at dinner. Perhaps the pictures that had appeared on his computer were to blame. Whatever the reason, Matthew Bourne found it difficult to sleep that night.

When eventually he did drift off, it seemed to be only a few minutes before he was lying wide-eyed and awake once more. The house was silent except for the ticking of the clock in the hall. It was surprisingly muggy for that time of the year and the sheets seemed clammy against Matthew's skin.

He glanced across the room at the computer which, only twenty-four hours ago, had been the pride of his life but which was now a

thing of mystery and maybe even fear. For a moment, he thought he saw an image appearing on the screen. He sat up sharply, then relaxed, feeling foolish. It was nothing but light from the corridor shining through the half-closed door of the bedroom.

He got up, closed the door, smoothed out the sheets of his bed and lay down again. Within five minutes, he was asleep.

It was at some point deep in the night that

something woke him. The room was much colder now and there was an odd, musty smell of dampness in the air. Someone must have opened the door because, although Matthew was facing the wall, there was light in the room.

He looked towards the door. It was closed.

Slowly, Matthew turned, knowing in his heart what he would see. Across the room, gazing at him as if it were an eye in the night, was the computer. It glowed green, the water on its screen shimmering and shivering as if a light breeze was troubling its surface.

His mouth dry, Matthew pushed back the duvet. He stood for a moment before his bed, a pale, illuminated figure. Then he moved towards the computer, forcing himself forward to the light. He looked deep into the image and saw, for the first time, a darkness – a sort of shadow – in the centre of the screen.

At that moment, the water seemed to become clearer and Matthew saw, as if it were daytime, as if it were real, what lay beneath the glittering surface.

It was the face of a human, a boy. His eyes were wide, his mouth moving soundlessly. The dark hair on the boy's head moved backwards and forwards like dark seaweed caressed by the tide.

Matthew sat down slowly on the stool, gazing deep into the screen. The boy was quite young – maybe eight or nine years old.

He seemed to be saying something, again and again, almost pleadingly.

Instinctively, Matthew's fingers touched the keyboard. He tapped out the letters:

What do you want?

And a sound, a whisper, reached him, coming not from the computer but from the cold air around him.

"*Don't . . . be . . . afraid . . .*"

Matthew gazed deep into the screen. He typed:

Who are you?

"*Child.*"

What kind of child?

"*Not child.*" The voice was clipped and precise – strangely old fashioned. "*Giles. Giles Casson.*"

Giles.

"*Help . . . me.*"

The room was filled with the sound of breathing – quick, uneven – like that of someone whose life was ebbing away.

Matthew's hands, clammy with fear, hesitated over the keyboard. He tapped in a single word.

How?

"*Shall we be friends? Do let's.*" The voice around him was faint, but almost playful. "*Shall we be friends?*"

Matthew noticed that the image on the screen seemed to be growing milky and indistinct, as if its energy was fading.

"*Shall we be . . .*" It was a whisper now, the sound of the wind in the walnut tree outside "*. . . friends?*"

The screen was dark, the room silent except for the sound of Matthew's own breathing. As if in a dream, he felt his way back to bed. He lay, staring upwards, the sound of his heart beating in his ears. Like a distant echo, within his mind or maybe outside it, the boy's voice was there, again and again.

"*Shall we be friends?*"

Chapter 5
Witch

Matthew spent the next day in a sort of daze. He said nothing at breakfast. When his dad drove him to school, he stared out of the window at the fields, the cattle, the dew on the hedgerows, the golden colours of autumn but seeing only the face of Giles Casson, hearing the pleading whisper of his voice.

"Are you all right?" his father asked.

"I'm fine."

"Not ill or anything?"

"No, honestly. I'm fine."

At school, he was unable to concentrate. As he sat at his desk that morning, the voice of Mrs Wheeler, the class teacher, seem to reach him through a long, echoing tunnel.

"Matthew? Matthew? *Matthew?*" she said at one point. "Are you with us this morning?"

"It was his birthday yesterday." Paul Knight, the biggest and meanest boy spoke up from the back of the class. "Maybe he's got a massive hangover."

Steve and Gavin, who liked to sit close to Paul and think of themselves as part of his gang, spluttered with false laughter.

Matthew ignored them. Paul Knight was one of those people who had an instinct for trouble, who could somehow sense unhappiness, and then liked to spread a bit more unhappiness around, to make the trouble worse.

Matthew looked down, aware that everyone in the class was looking at him. "Sorry, Mrs Wheeler," he murmured.

Angie caught up with him during the lunch break. She found him, sitting alone eating his sandwiches, in the dining room. "What's up, Matto?" she asked.

"Nothing."

She sat down opposite him. "Don't give me that. Something's happened, hasn't it – something with the computer?"

"You don't want to know."

"What exactly doesn't she want to know?"

The voice of Paul Knight echoed around the dining room. Followed by Steve and Gavin, he approached the table.

"What are the two class losers talking about then?" Paul stood, hand in pockets, jingling some coins.

"Leave us alone, Paul," said Angie.

"How's the old hangover, Matt?" Gavin asked, as if the joke was so good that it deserved a second outing.

Paul ambled round to Matthew's side of the table and sat beside him. "What's the problem, mate?" He smiled dangerously. "You seem a little down in the dumps today."

"I'm fine." Matthew spoke quietly.

"He's not feeling well," said Angie.

"Shut up, Mouse, I wasn't talking to you."
Paul spoke without taking his eyes off
Matthew. "I don't like it when someone's
down in the dumps." He placed a meaty hand
on the back of Matthew's neck. "I get down
in the dumps, too."

"Yeah, we get really sad," said Steve.

Paul was tightening his grip, pushing
Matthew's face down towards the table.

"Leave him alone, Paul," said Angie. "I'm warning you—"

At that moment Paul hesitated. Then, frowning slightly, he looked down at his right pocket. Smoke was coming from his trousers. A sharp, acrid smell like burning plastic filled the air. Suddenly, Paul gave a sort of yelp and leaped to his feet, thumping his thigh and dancing about. Eventually, he was able to reach into his pocket and take out his mobile phone. He dropped it on to the table where it lay, smoking slightly.

Everyone in the dining room gathered around. "My mobile." Paul's voice sounded more panicky than angry. "The screen's all blackened." He poked a button and, leaning over the phone, put his ear to it. "Dead," he said.

Slowly, as if replaying what had happened in his mind, he straightened and looked up at Angie. "Was that you?"

Angie was pale. "I didn't do anything," she said.

"She did and all." Gavin pushed forward. "She said, 'I'm warning you,' and suddenly the mobile was, like, *whooooofff* – burnt toast."

"She's a witch – I always said she was weird," said Steve.

"This is crazy," said Matthew. "Something must have been wrong with the phone. It was a coincidence."

But Paul ignored him. He blew on the phone, then returned it to his pocket. "You're going to pay for this, you witch," he said to Angie and marched out of the dining room, followed by Steve and Gavin.

Slowly, normality returned to the room. "That's all we need," said Angie gloomily. "Thicko Paul's mobile goes on the blink and I get the blame. Typical."

Matthew pushed away his plate. "I think maybe we should talk about last night," he said quietly.

There, as the dining room began to empty, he told her about being woken, about the water glowing on the screen, about the face, about Giles Casson, about what he had said, what he had wanted. After he had finished, Angie murmured, "Tell me again the words that he said."

"He just said, 'Help me'. Then, 'Shall we be friends?' – over and over again."

"You don't think that's what's going on now – that Paul's mobile was destroyed by this Giles, trying to be your friend?"

"If he can get into my computer, there's no reason why he shouldn't be able to mash up a mobile."

"That would mean he's here now." Angie looked around the empty dining room and shivered.

"And if he's decided that we're friends, where does that leave us?" Matthew spoke quietly. "What kind of help does he need?"

Chapter 6
The Murder Museum

Angie Wright did not believe in uncertainty. As far as she was concerned, a mystery was not so much mysterious as something that lacked the necessary facts to make it clear. So that evening, when she breezed into her flat, she knew exactly what she had to do.

"I'll be on the computer," she said, kissing her mum who was working in the spare room that doubled as an office.

"There's a surprise." Mrs Wright looked up from her paperwork and smiled. "What's the project now?"

"I need to help Matthew with something. His computer's sort of on the blink."

"Would you like to go over there?" Angie's

mother spoke casually. "I could give you a lift if you like. I . . . feel like a drive."

"No thanks, Mum. Not tonight."

Angie fetched a glass of orange from the fridge and went to her room. There was something niggling at the back of her mind and it was only as her computer came to life that she recognized what it was.

Her mother never wanted to take her anywhere after school, yet she had just volunteered to drive ten kilometres across the dark countryside. Something else about their conversation seemed a bit odd – a lightness in her mum's voice, a look in her eye.

Angie thought for a moment. Her mum and Mr Bourne? She shook her head. No. It was ridiculous. Mrs Wright hadn't been out with anyone since Angie's dad had left home over a year ago. The idea was crazy.

She went online and accessed her favourite search engine. She typed in the words "Giles Casson" and waited.

Facts. She needed the facts. With the facts, she would know exactly what to do next.

Two hours later, she emailed Matthew.

Matto123

I've done an Internet search for "Giles Casson". It turns out that there are loads of sites with that name and I almost gave up, but then I came across something called The Murder Museum.

If you can believe it, this is a website about "Murderers of the Twentieth Century". Giles Casson was there under the entry for someone called Joe Beglin who was jailed for killing two children in 1952. I've pasted what it says on the website here. Read this:

"... Beglin was suspected of committing other murders, including that of a nine-year-old boy called Giles Casson who disappeared while on holiday with his mother near Orford, Suffolk. Beglin was known to live in the area at the time but he always denied, up to his death in 1966, that he was responsible for the death of the child, whose body was never found."

There are no pictures and no other details. What do you think?

Angie

Chapter 7
Staverton Thicks

Giles was back.

It was after midnight. Matthew lay in bed, awake, his face turned to the wall. His eyes were closed but he sensed that the computer was alive, glowing in the darkness. Already the face would be there, staring out at him, waiting with watery intensity. It was cold in the room. A scent of decay, like that of a damp, dark cellar was in the air. Soon the voice, whispering and pleading, would be all around.

Like a sleepwalker, Matthew turned and rose from the bed. He walked to the computer and sat down, wide-eyed, before the screen. Tonight he somehow felt no fear, only gladness that his friend had returned. He raised his hands over the keyboard like a pianist at the beginning of a concert. He began to type.

Hi, Giles

A sort of sigh, heavy with relief, sounded in the air around him. "*You're here.*"

Giles, I need to ask you some questions.

"*You jolly well took your time. I was almost giving up on you.*"

Something weird happened at school. You know what it was, don't you?

For a moment, there was silence. "*Maybe.*" The word was spoken briefly, in a manner that was almost embarrassed.

Matthew typed:

Why did you do that, Giles?

"*It's what friends are for.*"

But why? I mean, why me?

This time there was long pause before the answer came.

"*We need each other. You will understand one day.*"

What do you want from me?

"*We want the truth. We want . . .*" the voice paused ". . . *peace.*"

Matthew sat back. Talking with a ghost was never going to be easy, but Giles seemed to be almost shy, as if he were a real little boy, afraid in the company of a stranger.

What do you mean? What truth?

Silence.

Giles?

"*The memories. They rather give me the creeps.*"

Matthew decided to take another approach.

Did you die in 1952?

A long, sad sigh seemed to fill the room. "*Twenty-ninth of November, nineteen fifty-two. We were out for a walk. There was water – water everywhere. Staverton Thicks.*"

As if exhausted by the effort, Giles stopped talking.

What's Staverton Thicks? Is it the

name of a person?

The sound of breathing seemed to grow louder. "*A place.*"

Matthew waited for a few seconds, then slowly typed the words:

Were you murdered?

A sort of sob could be heard.

Giles, please tell me. Matthew hammered at the keys. If I'm going to help you, you must tell me what happened.

The ghost was crying more loudly now, a terrible, dry, racking sound in the darkness.

Matthew typed again.

Was it murder?

There was a long intake of breath. Then a word, so loud that Matthew feared that his father or his sister would be woken, buffeted the air all around him.

"*MUMMY . . .*"

The screen grew darker, the sound of breathing faded. Giles Casson was gone.

"Mummy." Alone, Matthew said the word

out loud and, as he did so, he forgot about Giles and saw his own mother, Gemma Bourne, in the kitchen. The sun was shining through the window and she was smiling, looking down at him. Deep within him he felt a familiar lurch of grief and loneliness.

He shook his head. Things were confusing enough without thoughts of his own mother. He thought back to what Giles had said and remembered that there had been a question which had been bothering him but he had been unable to ask.

"We want the truth. We want peace," Giles had said. Truth, peace – Matthew could just about see that. But "we"? And why did he say, "*We* need each other?" What on earth could Matthew need from a ghost?

Chapter 8
Locked

Matthew discovered that losing sleep every night, sometimes for two or three hours, made him feel strange and out of sorts during the daytime. He talked little to his father or to Catherine. He spent more time with Angie but was really only happy when they were discussing Giles Casson, the ghost in his computer.

For Giles was not only in his computer, he was with Matthew all the time, in his thoughts and in his heart. Matthew spoke to him every night, learning small, interesting things about his life. Giles's father was an officer in the army and spent much of his time away from home. He was an only child and went to boarding school where, he admitted in a brave whisper, he sometimes felt lonely and homesick.

He had a dog called Jess. They lived in Suffolk near the seaside. Sometimes they went crabbing at Walberswick.

So it went on, this communication between human and ghost, boy and machine. Only when Matthew typed in certain words – "pop music" or "TV" – did the room go silent. Even "computer" and "mobile phone" confused Giles, as if he had no idea exactly how it was that he was talking to someone, only that it was happening – after fifty years of silence, it was happening at last.

With Giles beside him and within him, Matthew felt strong. They may have been different in character and background, they may have been separated by half a century of time, but when Giles spoke of being lonely, Matthew felt the emptiness within as if it were his own. When Giles talked of his mother, it was Matthew's own memories that came flooding back. When he talked of finding the truth, of discovering peace at last, Matthew began to understand what he meant.

The quest was no longer that of a ghost in his computer. It was his own. Giles and Matthew, Matthew and Giles. They were together, united.

Occasionally, at school, Matthew forgot this change within him. As if sensing the need to be reminded of his new self, Giles made his presence felt in various, strange ways.

Once, while Matthew was struggling during a class computer test having not prepared for it, the system went down and the test had to be abandoned. When Paul or one of his gang were paying him unwelcome attention, one of their mobile phones would ring. When it was answered, there would be the sound of breathing down the phone. Matthew over-heard Gavin complaining that his computer at home had started to behave oddly. On

another occasion, when he had logged on, a
message reading:

YOU HAVE GHOST MAIL

appeared on the screen. When he had double-
clicked on it, the screen had grown, the word
Boo! had loomed up followed, in smaller
letters, by ha ha ha ha.

"I could get used to this, to tell the truth,"
Angie said as they stood at the school gates at
the end of the day on Friday.

"Hm?" As usual, Matthew's thoughts had been with Giles. "Used to what?"

"Giles." Angie flicked a stick of chewing-gum into her mouth. "It's just great to know that he's there all the time, looking out for you."

"Yes." Matthew smiled. "It is."

"Kind of like having a ghost as a pet."

Matthew turned, his eyes dark against his pale skin. "What did you say?" he asked.

Angie held up both hands in mock surrender. "Er, maybe not a pet," she said quickly.

"He's my friend," said Matthew.

"OK," said Angie. "Sheesh, you're weirding me out these days, Matto."

Matthew looked away. "A true friend," he murmured under his breath, sensing in a moment that what Giles brought him, a connection to an easier, happier past, a time when his mother was still alive, now meant more to him than almost anything – even his friendship with Angie.

"Ready then?" The voice of his father

brought Matthew out of his reverie.

"Hi, Dad," he said.

"Hullo, Angie," said Mr Bourne as Matthew stepped into the car. "How's your mother these days?"

Angie smiled politely. "She's fine."

"Give her my best regards."

"Er, OK. I'll do that, Mr Bourne." Angie glanced doubtfully at Matthew.

Matthew stared back as if he had seen or heard nothing.

"This has got to stop."

Mr Bourne spoke in his best serious-father voice as they pulled away from the school.

"Sorry?" asked Matthew.

"I've had enough of all this mooning about. I can't think what's come over you this week and nor can Catherine."

"I'm OK, Dad."

"Mrs Wheeler's noticed, too. She's sent me a note."

Matthew stared silently out of the window.

"She says you've given up paying attention in lessons. She's worried about the way you're looking."

Matthew shrugged.

"It's that computer, isn't it?" Mr Bourne looked in the rear-view mirror, catching Matthew's eye before he looked away quickly. "I don't know what you've been doing with it, but I've had enough. It's got to stop."

"OK," said Matthew.

"No, it's not OK," said Mr Bourne. "I've taken it out of your room and locked it in the storeroom."

"No," Matthew whispered. "No, Dad, please."

"Pull yourself together, start doing your homework and pay attention at school. Then we can talk about the computer."

Chapter 9
Scream

Catherine and Matthew Bourne had discovered one thing about their father over the past four years. On the rare occasions when he decided to be firm, there was no weakening or changing his mind. In the old days, their mum used to tell him he was too soft with the children – "They wrap you round their little fingers," she would say – and at the time it was true. Now that he was the only parent, he seemed to hear her voice now and then and have to prove to them and to himself that he was in charge.

"Please, Dad." Matthew looked up at his father from his bed that night. "Please give me back the computer. I need it."

Mr Bourne glanced across the room to the table where the Epsilon had been. "Let's have one computer-free weekend," he said. "We can talk. You can do your homework. Maybe we can go on some sort of outing on Sunday."

"It's important, Dad. You don't understand."

His father smiled. "What I understand is that you're very tired. We've got to break the spell of that machine."

"It's more than a machine," Matthew said quietly.

Mr Bourne looked down at his son, smoothing the hair out of his eyes in a gentle movement. "Is there something you would like to tell me? Something's been going on, hasn't it?"

Matthew thought of Giles Casson and, in a brief moment of longing, he wanted to tell his father everything that had happened over the past week but, knowing that it would all sound crazy, he shook his head.

"I'm fine," he said, turning his face to the wall.

His father kissed his head, then turned off the bedside lamp. "'Night, Matt," he said. "You'll feel better when you've had some sleep."

Matthew awoke as usual at the dead of night but this time when he opened his eyes, the room was not glowing softly, there was not the familiar chill in the air. Darkness was all around.

He slipped out of bed and sat on the stool in front of the computer table.

"Giles?" he whispered. "Can you hear me?"

Silence.

"I'll reach you soon." Matthew spoke more loudly now. "I won't leave you, I promise."

Again he waited. Again there was no sound from the gloom around him.

Slowly, he returned to his bed. He lay down and stared into the darkness, feeling a terrible emptiness within. He wiped his eyes, which seemed to have filled with tears. "I'm sorry, Giles," he whispered. Soon he was asleep.

A scream cut the night air.

Matthew sat up sharply, his senses on full alert.

"Daddy!" Catherine was calling out but the fear in her voice made her sound more like a little girl than a teenager. Matthew switched on the bedside light. He heard footsteps running into Catherine's room, then his father's soothing tones.

Matthew stepped out of bed and made his way quickly down the corridor.

Catherine was sitting up in bed, staring wordlessly across the room to the corner where her work desk was. On it was her laptop computer. Its screen was black and had shattered outwards as if some missile had been thrown from within it.

"There was this loud buzzing sound," said Catherine. "It woke me. The screen of the computer was white – it dazzled my eyes. Then suddenly it sort of . . . exploded."

"It's all right, love." Mr Bourne put an arm round his daughter's shoulders. "It was just an electrical fault."

"It can't be." Panic had returned to Catherine's voice. "I turned the computer off at the mains before I went to bed. I always do that."

"You must have forgotten." Mr Bourne crossed the room and knelt down by the desk, examining the mains switch. "How very strange," he said. "It does seem to be switched off."

"How could that happen?" Catherine whispered.

"There must be an explanation," said Mr Bourne.

Standing at the door, Matthew was about to speak. Then, from downstairs, the telephone began to ring.

For what seemed an age, the three members of the Bourne family were frozen into immobility, Matthew standing at the door, Catherine sitting up in bed, their father kneeling on the floor. During those seconds, as the phone echoed through the house, each of them was caught up in the same terrible memory – of the call, four years ago, that had changed their lives for ever. Since that terrible time, the ring of the telephone at night at Walnut Tree Farm had represented tragedy.

Now, from downstairs, something else could be heard – something that made the hairs on the back of Matthew's neck rise like the fur of a frightened cat. It was the sound, quiet but unmistakable, of human voices talking.

"What's going on?" Catherine whispered.

Mr Bourne stood up. "Some sort of practical joke, I expect," he said, walking quickly to the door. "Someone's having a laugh at our expense."

Matthew and Catherine heard him pick up the phone in the hall downstairs. "Hullo?" he said. "Hullo?" He put the receiver down. Moments later, the voices were gone.

"Nothing to worry about," he said when he returned to Catherine's room. "There was just a dialling tone when I picked up. And someone must have left the TV on."

"I'm frightened," said Catherine. "It's as if we're being attacked through our appliances."

"Some kind of computer error in the electrical system." Mr Bourne smiled but he looked pale and wary, as if he were wondering from where the next nasty surprise would come. "I'll sort it out in the morning. Let's all get some sleep."

"Don't go, Dad." Catherine spoke quietly.

"I'll leave the light on in the corridor." He glanced at Matthew. "Are you all right, Matt?"

"I'm fine," said Matthew. He noticed something behind his father. Catherine's mobile phone was on her desk beside the shattered laptop. "Maybe we should take the mobile out of the room," he said.

"Too right," muttered Catherine.

"I'll put it on the hall table." Matthew picked up the mobile. It was warm and seemed to tremble like a scared animal.

"Is it all right?" Catherine asked.

"It's fine." Matthew smiled, finding the lie came easily to him.

In the corridor outside, Mr Bourne murmured to Matthew, "Thanks for being so grown-up. It's easy to get spooked when these things happen."

"I don't spook easy. I'll put the mobile downstairs, then."

He watched his father close his door behind him. Then, without a moment's hesitation, he returned to his room. He slipped into bed and looked down at the mobile that he held in the palm of his hand. He pressed the "On" button.

The screen read:

you have 5276 missed messages

Matthew laughed softly. "Easy, Giles," he said. "No need to go mad."

He pressed the "Return call" button. A

series of zeros appeared on the screen. There was a brief sound of ringing, then silence.

He typed in the text message:

ru there giles? and waited for the reply.

The room grew chilly. Matthew coughed briefly at the smell of dampness.

He keyed in, more slowly this time:

i rpt ru there?

The air around him seemed to stir as if an invisible presence were moving through it. "*Roo?*" said a voice, so close to Matthew that it seemed almost part of him. "*What does 'roo' mean? What's a 'rpt'?*"

Matthew smiled.

ru there is a text message it means are you there

There was a moment's hesitation, as if the ghost were trying to understand the idea of text-messaging. Then the voice returned. "*Bally odd world you've got there,*" it said.

thanks giles

Matthew thumbed.

you scared the hell out of us

"Don't blame me – I needed to talk to you."
Giles's voice was louder now.

no need to be in such a temper about it

An odd sound, like a sort of ghostly cough,
could be heard and Matthew realized that
Giles Casson was laughing. *"You'd be in a
temper if you had waited for fifty years to talk
to someone,"* he said.

Matthew carefully keyed in the words:

what dyou want from me?

*"On Sunday, you must go to Staverton
Thicks. You will know what to do."*

why?

For a moment, there was silence. Then, *"I
want you to meet me. Together, we must save
my mother."*

how giles. what's happening? Matthew paused.

im your friend

"Do . . . it." The words were like a long,
slow breath. *"Do . . . it . . . for . . . me."*

Chapter 10
Strong

There was a strange atmosphere in the Bourne household the next morning. Catherine was hollow-eyed and pale. Never at her best over breakfast, today she was more snappy and impatient than usual, as if she were both annoyed with herself at having been scared during the night and yet still slightly afraid. Mr Bourne was brisk, distracted. Normally on Saturday mornings, he would do a few hours' work on the farm but today, he announced over breakfast, he would remain at home to check whether there was anything wrong with the house's electrical appliances.

Matthew, on the other hand, felt good. He

70

knew in his heart that last night the Bourne family had not been threatened by danger and mystery but had merely been visited by a friend. It was coming, he knew it – the moment of truth, of peace. Soon, perhaps the very next day, the emptiness would be gone, the waiting would be over. He longed to share his happiness with the others but he knew that, just for a few hours more, it must remain a secret.

After breakfast, he found his father in the small room beneath the stairs examining the controls for the central heating.

"Can't think what was going on last night," Mr Bourne muttered as he fiddled with the dials. "All the timings seem to have been changed."

"It was nothing, Dad," said Matthew. "Just one of those things that happen."

"Yes," said Mr Bourne uncertainly. "I suppose it was."

"By the way . . ." Matthew tried, without much success, to sound casual. "Have you ever heard of a place called Staverton Thicks?"

Mr Bourne continued tinkering. "It's a wood – about half an hour away from here. Doing a field trip there, are you?"

"No, but Mrs Wheeler mentioned it the other day. I thought it sounded really interesting."

"What is this, Matthew?" Mr Bourne stopped working for a moment. "What are you up to now?"

"I was just thinking that it might be a good

place to go on that family outing you mentioned – tomorrow, maybe." Matthew's voice sounded unconvincing, even to him.

His father laughed. "Nice joke, Matt. What d'you really want? It's something to do with that computer, isn't it?"

"I'm serious, Dad. I want to go to Staverton Thicks."

His father sighed. "It's a bit of a way, isn't it? I'll have to check with Catherine."

"I've asked her. She wants to revise here." He paused. "Maybe we could take Angie. Perhaps Mrs Wright might like to come along."

Mr Bourne frowned but a small smile had appeared on his lips. "I suppose I'm not that busy," he said casually. "An outing with the four of us – you, Angie, me and Sandy."

Something about the way his father spoke the name of Angie's mother, as if the word "Sandy" contained a special kind of magic only he understood, made Matthew smile.

"Thanks, Dad," he said.

Chapter 11
Life is but a Dream

Anyone seeing Stephen Bourne's beaten-up Ford making towards the Suffolk coast that morning might have assumed that its four passengers were a regular family on a Sunday outing. Sandra Wright was in the front passenger seat chatting animatedly to Mr Bourne. Angie and Matthew sat behind them, neither of them talking, each silent for their own reasons.

It had been a surprise to Angie quite how nervous her mother had been at the idea of spending the day with the Bournes. She had worried over what to wear, giggly and tense as if this was some kind of date rather than a picnic in the forest. Angie found this surprisingly irritating. She liked the way her mother and herself had become a team of two but now it suddenly occurred to her that what she found good and normal must make her mother feel lonely. It was almost as if having a daughter was not enough to make her happy.

"For goodness' sake, Mum, it's only Mr Bourne," she had said as her mother fussed with her hair in front of the hall mirror.

"There's nothing wrong with trying to make yourself look nice, you know," Mrs Wright had said briskly. Angie sensed criticism in the words and this had made her feel even grumpier.

Now, as she sat in the back of Mr Bourne's car, Angie sighed. In front, the adults were chatting away as if they had forgotten that their children existed. As for Matthew, he seemed to grow stranger and less like himself with every day that passed. It was as if he had been drifting off into some kind of trance.

Why was it that everyone had suddenly gone weird on her?

*

Against the blur of trees racing by outside he caught the reflection of his face in the car window. His hair was dark and combed with a neat parting, his face small and solemn. Matthew smiled and the shimmering, half-visible image in the window smiled, too. He was staring into the eyes of Giles Casson.

They drove into the depths of the forest where tall trees bent in the blustery wind. At one point, Matthew's father suggested that they might pay a visit to a pub in Snape.

"How about that, Angie?" asked Mrs Wright, glancing over her shoulder.

"Whatever," said Angie.

"Staverton Thicks," said Matthew, and he was surprised to hear that something in his voice seemed to have changed. "We must go there first. You can jolly well go to your pub later."

Mr Bourne glanced in the mirror. "Are you all right, Matthew?" he asked.

"Of course I bally am," said Matthew.

"You're talking in a really weird accent, Matt," said Angie but Matthew, staring out of the window, seemed not to hear her.

Ten minutes later, the car turned off a small road down a track into a dark and gloomy wood. After about half a kilometre, the lane came to an end outside a small wooden hut.

They stepped out of the car, the four of them. Mr Bourne walked to a plastic map by

the entrance to the hut. "Where to, boss?" he called out jokingly to his son.

Matthew looked around him uncertainly.

"There are tables inside," said Mrs Wright, looking through one of the hut windows. "Let's have a quick bite, then go for a walk afterwards. How about that, Angie?"

Angie shrugged and looked away.

They entered the hut and, as Angie and

Matthew looked out of the window, the two parents laid out the sandwiches.

"I'm going to have a dekko," said Matthew in his odd, bright new voice.

"A dekko?" murmured Angie. "What's a dekko when it's at home?"

"Why don't you both go?" asked Mrs Wright. "Work up a bit of an appetite?"

Angie smiled coldly as if to say that she was all too aware that what was on her mother's mind was nothing to do with appetite or food but the chance of being alone with Matthew's dad for a few moments. "I'm staying here," she said. "It looks lame out there."

"Are you sure, love?" said Mrs Wright, a flicker of irritation crossing her face. "Matthew would like the company."

Angie glanced at the door which Matthew had closed firmly behind him. "Yeah, right."

Outside, alone, Matthew had already forgotten the hut, his father, Angie and her mother.

His eyes gazed into the tangled greenery of the forest.

"Mummy," he whispered. He walked with quick, determined steps towards one of the three paths that led away from the clearing. Within moments, he had stepped into the darkness of the woods and was gone.

The day was not going at all the way Angie had hoped it would. She gazed out of the window into the trees as, behind her, the adults chatted away to one another, ignoring her presence entirely. So far as Angie could tell, they were talking about cattle. Once or twice, she was unable to resist glancing over her shoulder, so that her mother realized that at least one person in that hut knew what a fool she was making of herself. When Mr Bourne and Mrs Wright had continued talking, she sighed loudly.

"Why don't you go and see what Matthew's up to?" her mum asked brightly.

"Er, why exactly?" Angie muttered.

"A bit of exercise might improve your mood, young lady."

Angie screwed up her face and silently mimicked her mother's words. She hated it when her mum tried to behave like a regular parent in front of other adults.

"Actually, Matthew's been out there a while," said Mr Bourne. "Maybe you could check what he's up to."

Angie thought about it for a moment. Then, shrugging, she walked gloomily out of the hut.

The wind seemed to have grown stronger over the past few minutes and, as soon as she stepped outside, Angie felt the spots of rain on her face. When she called Matthew's name, her voice seemed muffled and lost.

She called again, louder. The wind moaned through the trees.

Angie felt the first, faint sense of alarm. She thought back to what happened that day, remembering how pale Matthew had looked, the weird, unfocused expression in his eyes, the odd half-smile that flickered across his face now and then, as if he were in possession of a secret that no one else, not even she, could ever guess, the way he had starting speaking, like someone out of an old black-and-white film.

Then it came to her, a terrible thought.

What if Giles Casson was not good at all but bad – evil? What if those sessions late at night, the messages on the computer, the tricks played on the mobile phones of guys at school, were all ways of winning Matthew's confidence, of drawing him into something from which he was unable to escape?

"It was a trap." Angie spoke the words out loud. That was why Matthew had been drawn to this desolate place miles away from anywhere and that was why, now, he had walked off, disappeared. He was somewhere out there in the forest, alone, being brought closer and closer to the spirit of Giles Casson.

She turned, sprinted up the steps and burst into the hut.

"It's Matthew!" she shouted. "Something's happened. We've got to save him before it's too late."

Matthew walked, eyes fixed on the shadowy, narrow path ahead of him. Now and then whip-like branches stung his face, brambles tugged at his coat like fingers trying to hold him back, but he noticed none of it.

He reached a clearing and hesitated, briefly uncertain where he should go. He looked up and saw clouds, grey and threatening, racing low over the trees. It had begun to rain. He threw back his head and let the water run down his face. He laughed, an odd, unearthly sound in the restless, gusting wind. He loved water. Water was his friend. It was his destiny.

To the right of him he saw a gap in the undergrowth. It was not so much a path as a hole used by deer and foxes. Its darkness drew Matthew forward.

He lowered his head and entered. A bramble caught his cheek and tore the flesh and, for a moment, the pain made Matthew stop. He touched his face, then looked at his hand. Rain splashed the bright red of his blood.

He walked on, more slowly now. The forest was darker and thicker here as if no human had ever been there before.

Just then he heard a sound above the wind. At first he thought it was his imagination but, when he stopped and stood still among the trees, it became more distinct. It was the voice of a woman. She seemed to be singing.

"Mummy?" he called.

Fearful, yet knowing that to turn back was impossible, he moved forward. There was a bend in the path and, as Matthew turned round a tall oak, he saw that he was no longer alone.

"Mummy?"

In front of him, where the path widened, was a figure in an old, dark-blue coat, walking slowly ahead of him on the path. It was hunched and so small that he might have taken it to be a child were it not for the lank, wet, grey hair that lay flattened by the rain on its head and shoulders.

The voice, its thin, reedy tones cutting through the moaning wind, was clear enough for Matthew to be able to tell that she was singing a sort of lullaby.

"Row, row, row your boat
Gently down the stream . . ."

The old woman took several breaths before continuing, more loudly this time.

"Merrily, merrily, merrily, merrily,
Life is but a dream."

Matthew stood still as the figure wandered away from him. The woman muttered something to herself, then began the song again. This time the voice was strangely gentle, like that of a mother singing her baby to sleep.

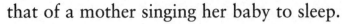

"*Row, row, row your boat*
Gently down the—"

Suddenly she stopped, as if something very important had just occurred to her. Then, to Matthew's choking, wordless horror, she began to turn towards him.

For a few seconds, as the two of them faced one another on the path, it seemed as if the woman had not seen him. Then, in the pallid folds of her face, the eyes widened. She raised her stick-like arms towards him and, with a sound that seemed to shake the trees around them, she screamed a single word.

"*GILES!*"

"No." Matthew began to back away, shaking his head. When the woman began walking towards him, he shouted it more loudly. "No! You're not my mother."

But the sound of Matthew's voice seemed only to encourage the woman. "My Giles," she said and, as she drew closer, Matthew could see that she was smiling and sobbing at the same time.

He tried to back away but the forest seemed to have closed in behind him, holding him there. He turned and plunged through the undergrowth, tearing and lashing with

his hand at the thorny branches.

"*Giles! stay, please!*"

He heard the old woman's desperate wail. Closing his eyes, he battled onwards, choking with fear and disappointment, pursued by the voice behind him.

It must have been two or three minutes before he dared to slow down. Then, breathing heavily, he looked around him. In his terror he had left the narrow path and had made his way further into the densest part of the forest, losing any sense of direction, knowing only that he must flee from that voice.

To his left, he noticed something. Through a break in the trees, the landscape seemed to change. Beyond the damp browns of the forest, a stretch of green – as bright as a cricket pitch on a perfect summer's afternoon – glimmered like a welcome light in the darkness.

He walked towards it, aware for the first time that his hands and wrists had been lacerated by thorns and brambles. Pushing aside a curtain of foliage, he stepped into the open and smiled with relief.

He had reached a narrow clearing. A trail of lush greenery led away from him towards – he was somehow sure – a main path and safety. Freed from the forest tangle, he could escape the old woman.

It was at that moment that he noticed something moving at the far end of the clearing. It was a small figure – one that he was sure that he recognized. "Giles?" he said. "Is that you?"

But his voice, weak and breathless, must have been lost in the wind, for the figure stood motionless for a moment, then slowly turned and melted back into the dark trees behind it.

"Giles!" Gathering what was left of his strength, Matthew ran headlong into the clearing. "Don't leave me—"

Suddenly, the ground was no longer there. As if the earth had opened up beneath him, Matthew fell downwards, plunging, choking, and when he gasped it was not air that entered his mouth, but water.

He flailed his arms in the dark, cold water but the more he tried to reach the surface, the more the green mantle of weed entangled him and pulled him downwards.

He opened his eyes and there, beneath the water, as his arms and his legs grew weak, Matthew understood.

The green. The shimmering darkness. He knew it and recognized it. His body was limp. The water rushed inwards and he welcomed it as it became part of him and he became part of it.

At last, he was there.

He was with Giles.

He was Giles.

He was home.

It was Angie who first heard the cry.

"What was that?" she said, standing on the path. Her mother and Mr Bourne stopped walking. This time they all heard it.

"It sounds like a woman crying," said Angie's mum. "What's she doing here?"

"She's saying something," said Mr Bourne. "Repeating one word."

Angie listened. "It's 'Giles' – that's what she's saying." Angie began running in the direction of the voice. "She'll know where Matthew is."

Mr Bourne was first to reach the clearing. He stopped, panting, when he saw an old woman standing on the far side, swaying, repeating the same word again and again.

"Have you seen a boy?" Mr Bourne called out, as Angie and her mother arrived.

The woman ignored him.

"Where's Giles?" Angie screamed. "Where's Giles Casson?"

Now the woman looked up, her eyes wide with horror. Then, slowly, she extended her arm. With a shaking, bony finger, she pointed to a spot in front of her where, in a small parting in the greenery, the glint of dark water could be seen.

"Oh my God!" shouted Angie. "It's water. He's in there!"

Mr Bourne was already stumbling forward, plunging into the green, downwards into the dark water.

Chapter 12
Released

One more minute. Sixty seconds later and it would have been too late. For the rest of his life, Matthew would remember how near he had once been to ending his days in the depths of a treacherous hidden pond in Staverton Thicks.

After his father had dragged him from the pond, revived him with the kiss of life and rushed him to hospital, Matthew was kept in overnight for observation. The human body takes a while to recover from shock and intense cold, the doctor told him.

The following morning, while Matthew was still feeling stiff and tired, his father visited him in the children's ward. It was the duckweed that had nearly killed him, Mr Bourne said. A plant that grew on the surface of ponds and looked dangerously like fresh grass, it was known as Creeping Jenny. It had been lucky that the old woman had been there to call out for help. She had been taken to the same hospital, suffering from cold and general confusion.

Creeping Jenny. Matthew smiled weakly. So that had been what Giles was going on about.

Later that day, during the afternoon, he was awoken from a light sleep by someone calling his name. When he opened his eyes, he found a stranger sitting on the chair by his bed. He was a tall, middle-aged man with the sorrowful expression of someone who has had to give too much bad news in his time.

"Hello, Matthew." The man put on a smile. "Sorry to wake you but I need a quick word before I return to the station. My name is Mullen – Detective Sergeant Mullen."

"Hello."

"There's nothing for you to worry about."
Casually, Mullen took a small notepad and
pencil from the inside pocket of his jacket. "It
was about your accident in the forest."

"Accident, yes." Matthew spoke carefully.

"The lady who saw you fall in the pond has
had her own tragedy." The policeman spoke
quietly. "Her name is Mrs Casson and fifty
years ago she lost her son."

Matthew nodded.

"At the time, it was believed that the boy was murdered. Now, half a century later, we know what happened to young Master Casson."

"Creeping Jenny," said Matthew quietly.

"He fell in the pond that nearly cost you your life. That was why, by some weird chance, Mrs Casson was in the area. She returns every year to the place where her son disappeared."

"I think she was searching for him," said Matthew.

"A police diving team went to work in the pond this morning. Certain . . . remains have been found, tangled in the weed."

"Giles."

"It was the remains of a child, yes." The policeman jotted something on his pad. "I wanted to warn you because there may be one or two journalists nosing around, asking questions."

Matthew nodded.

"As it happens, Mrs Casson was asking to see you," said the detective. "She's in a private room, next to Sherwood Ward on the next floor. Maybe you should call in before you go home."

"She wants to see me?"

"Of course, it's up to you." Mullen closed his notepad and returned it to his pocket. "If it upsets you, I can tell her you've gone home."

"No. I'll see her."

The detective stood up. "By the way," he said. "How did you know the Casson boy's name was Giles?"

Matthew smiled innocently. "You mentioned it earlier. Can't you remember?"

"Did I?" Detective Sergeant Mullen frowned uncertainly. "Did I really?"

Matthew watched the policeman go, then stepped out of bed and put on his dressing gown and slippers.

It was time to see Mrs Casson.

*

She lay in her bed, a small and fragile figure. For a moment as he stood at the door, Matthew wondered how this tiny woman, this smudge of grey against the white sheets, had managed to terrify and drive him almost to his death.

"Mrs Casson?" He spoke gently and the old woman's eyes flickered open, as if she had been expecting him.

"Oh." She smiled weakly. "How lovely."

Matthew walked into the room and sat on a chair beside Mrs Casson's bed. For a moment they looked at each other in silence. "I wanted to thank you," she said eventually.

"I should be thanking you," said Matthew. "If it hadn't been for you—" He stopped, seeing the look of impatience on the old woman's face.

"You freed me," she said softly. "After all these years, you have released me from the ghosts of the past. Because of you, I now know what happened to my son."

"Poor Giles," said Matthew.

"It was almost as if something guided you to me," said Mrs Casson. "Fate, maybe." Mrs Casson gazed upwards at the ceiling. "He was such a special little boy," she said, smiling. "He had a wonderful sense of humour."

Matthew thought back to the night when his Epsilon had been locked up, when Catherine's laptop had exploded. In his mind he heard a whisper, *Bally odd world you've got there*, followed by that strange, ghostly laugh. "I bet he was quite something, your Giles," he said.

Mrs Casson turned, a look of surprise on her face. "You know, he was – quite something. Once he set his mind on something, he was jolly well going to make sure that it happened."

"I can believe that," said Matthew.

"There was something else I wanted to tell you." With some difficulty, Mrs Casson pulled herself up in the bed. "As a sort of thank you, I'm going to send your father a cheque to put into savings for you. It won't be much – a thousand pounds – but it might be useful one day."

"That's really kind but—"

Mrs Casson reached for Matthew's hand and held it with surprising strength. "My son was not the only member of the family to be determined," she said quietly. "If you don't want the money, you can give it to charity."

"But why?"

"It was what Giles would have wanted. Somehow I can sense that." The old woman smiled. "He was a kind boy, like you."

A nurse tapped Matthew on the shoulder, "Your dad's waiting for you in the children's ward," she said. "He's come to take you home."

Politely, Matthew said goodbye to Mrs Casson and walked slowly back towards the stairs and back to his ward.

*

When Matthew returned home from the hospital later that afternoon it was as if he had been away for a long time, that he needed to be reminded of how normal life at home could be.

For some reason he had been reluctant to share with his father the details of his conversation with Mrs Casson but now, as Mr Bourne sat at the kitchen table paying the month's bills, he told him about the thousand pounds.

"Poor old dear." Matthew's father shook his head. "It must be the shock. We'd better quietly give the money to charity."

"I was thinking about Catherine," said Matthew. "She needs a new computer for her studies."

"I can't for the life of me see what that has to do with the old woman."

Matthew remembered the word Mrs Casson had used in the hospital. "It's fate, Dad," he said.

Something in his son's voice made Mr Bourne look up from his papers. "If you say so, Matt. It's your money," he said. "You're big enough to make this kind of decision yourself."

"I've decided."

"Oh, by the way." Matthew's father glanced at his watch. "Angie said she'd call round to see you on her way back from school."

"Angie and Sandy?"

"Yes," said Mr Bourne, smiling. "I rather think Sandy will be there, too."

Half an hour later, Matthew and Angie were climbing the stairs to his room. "Suddenly Dad's really keen on me checking my computer," Matthew grumbled jokily. "Particularly when your mum's around."

Angie laughed. "Yeah, and my mum can hardly get to the end of a sentence without mentioning your dad – it's Stephen this and Stephen that, all day long."

"I got the impression you weren't too keen on all that."

Angie pushed the door into Matthew's room. "So maybe I'm changing my mind. I watched them yesterday – the way they helped each other after you had gone into hospital. Suddenly I thought, you know, it's weird but this might actually work. In fact . . ." Angie frowned as if she were amazed by what she was saying ". . . it's kind of sweet in a way. Shall we check out the computer?"

Matthew glanced across the room at the Epsilon. "Maybe later," he said.

"You're scared that Giles Casson might still be in there somewhere, aren't you?"

Matthew sat on the stool in front of the computer and gazed for a moment at the dark screen. "It's not that," he said. "In fact, if anything, I'm scared that he won't be there."

"There's only one way to find out." Angie leaned forward and pressed the power switch.

The screen of the Epsilon brightened into life.

When Matthew double-clicked to go online, the machine seemed to flicker hesitantly.

Just then, in that moment, Matthew felt the room grow chillier, the air fill with the familiar scent of decay.

But Angie was smiling with relief. "Nothing wrong with that computer," she said.

Matthew listened. There, in the bedroom all around him, was a whisper, long and low, like a fading breath. "*Goodbye, Matthew.*" Then, "*Thank you.*"

"Bye, Giles," Matthew murmured.

"Eh?" Angie looked around. "Who are you talking to, Matto?"

"Can't you hear it?"

For a few seconds, the two of them sat in silence. From downstairs, they heard the front door opening, Catherine calling out on her return from school, and the voices, first of Mr Bourne, then of Mrs Wright, as they greeted her in the kitchen.

"Just sounds like life to me," said Angie.

Matthew looked around him. The air seemed to be warmer now. The welcome smell of home filled his nostrils.

"Yes," he said. "It sounds like life."